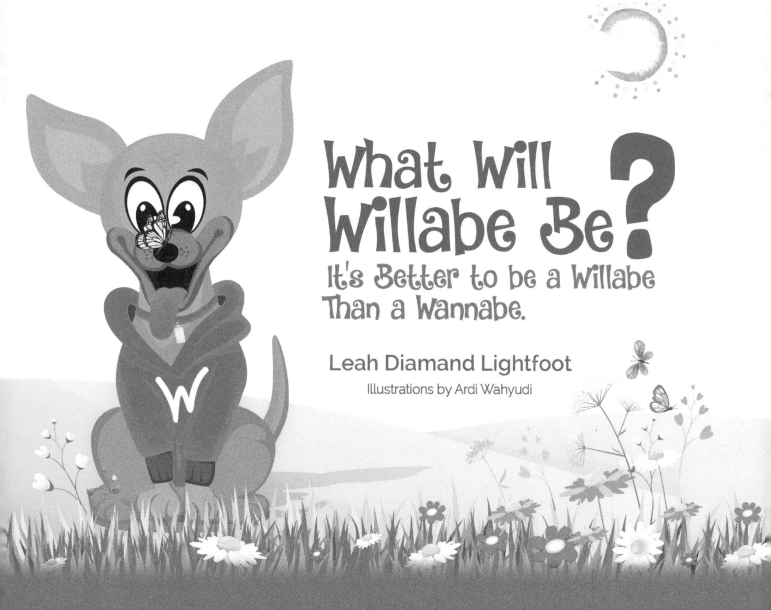

What Will Willabe Be?

It's Better to be a Willabe Than a Wannabe.

Leah Diamand Lightfoot

Illustrations by Ardi Wahyudi

AuthorHouse™
1663 Liberty Drive
Bloomington, IN 47403
www.authorhouse.com
Phone: 1 (800) 839-8640

Because of the dynamic nature of the Internet, any web addresses or links contained in this book may have changed since publication and may no longer be valid. The views expressed in this work are solely those of the author and do not necessarily reflect the views of the publisher, and the publisher hereby disclaims any responsibility for them.

Any people depicted in stock imagery provided by Getty Images are models, and such images are being used for illustrative purposes only.
Certain stock imagery © Getty Images.

This book is printed on acid-free paper.

ISBN: 978-1-7283-4893-3 (sc)
ISBN: 978-1-7283-4894-0 (hc)
ISBN: 978-1-7283-4892-6 (e)

Library of Congress Control Number: 2020904053

Print information available on the last page.

Published by AuthorHouse 02/27/2020

authorHOUSE

Dedication

This book is dedicated to my father.

Willabe was inspired by Shiloh, a dear little dog who passed on to the Rainbow Bridge in 2019.

Meet Willabe, a very happy dog.

Every day, Willabe went to the dog park and played with all the other happy dogs.

On the way, guess what happened?

A butterfly appeared and landed on Willabe's nose! Willabe smiled and said. "Well hello there! What is your name?"

The butterfly looked at Willabe and spread her wings.

"You are so very pretty. I will call you Bibi. Bibi the Butterfly!" exclaimed Willabe.

Bibi fluttered her wings in happiness.

From then on, they became instant friends and Bibi never left Willabe's side.

One day, a new dog came to the dog park.
His name is Wannabe.

Wannabe made friends and talked and talked
about everything he wanted to be.

The first day, Wannabe said proudly, "I want to be a herding dog! A herding dog keeps animals together so they don't get lost."

The second day, Wannabe said, "I want to be a guard dog for a firehouse! A guard dog is important because he makes sure everything is safe at the firehouse."

The third day, Wannabe said, "I want to be a police dog! A police dog is important because he helps the police catch the bad guys."

Willabe listened to Wannabe with much interest and thought about what he had to say. He finally asked Wannabe, "Well, if you want to be all of these things, then why aren't you doing them?"

This angered Wannabe because no one had ever asked him such a question. Wannabe did not really have a good answer. He only snarled at Willabe and shouted, "Because I have never tried!"

This answer would just not do for Willabe.
It would not do at all.

Willabe went home and thought about all of this.
He asked himself, "What do I want to be?"

Willabe thought and thought and decided it's
better to be a Willabe than a Wannabe

So what will Willabe be?

Summer had come and Willabe and his family were going on vacation to see Grandma and Grandpa! Yay! Grandma and Grandpa lived on a farm. They had all kinds of animals on the farm... chickens, goats, cows, pigs, horses, and geese. They even had sheep!

So off they drove to Grandma and Grandpa's house. When they finally got there, Willabe jumped out of the car, very happy to be running and playing. And all the new smells! With nose to the ground, Willabe started sniffing away.

Sniffing and running, sniffing and running. Finally, Willabe stopped and looked up and saw a long wooden fence. Inside the fence were lots of sheep. And a dog! A really big, white, fluffy dog!

Willabe watched the dog for a while and saw him running around the sheep, zigging and zagging. Willabe realized that this dog was working. He had a job to do! He was rounding the sheep up and keeping them all together.

The big, white, fluffy dog saw Willabe and ran up to the fence.

Willabe said, "Hello. My name is Willabe!"

The fluffy dog answered back and said, "Hello, Willabe, my name is Jake."

Willabe asked Jake, "Why do you run around the sheep like that?"

Jake explained, "To keep all the sheep together so they don't run off and get lost."

Willabe thought a moment and asked, "Is this your job? Is this what you do?"

Jake replied, "Yes, this is my job. I am a herding dog, and I have a purpose."

Willabe asked Jake, "Do you think I could be a herding dog?"

Jake said, "Well, let's give it a try."

So Willabe crawled under the fence and followed Jake towards the sheep. Willabe ran around the sheep, following Jake, but just couldn't run as fast.

Willabe was pooped!

Jake saw the disappointment in Willabe's eyes, and said, "Well, at least you tried. Maybe there is something else you can be."

Willabe agreed. "Goodbye, Jake,"

Jake replied, "Goodbye, Willabe."

That night, Willabe thought about
Jake and how fast he could run.
He really did his job well.

I will keep trying, Willabe decided,
because it's better to be a Willabe
than a Wannabe.

So what will Willabe be?

The next day, Willabe went into town with the family. He walked along the sidewalk and came upon a fire station. Willabe peered inside and saw a white dog with black spots.

He stopped for a moment and finally said to the dog, "Hello. My name is Willabe!"

The spotted dog came up to him and said, "Hello, Willabe, my name is Ruby!"

Willabe asked Ruby, "What do you do here?"

Ruby answered, "I guard the firehouse and equipment."

Willabe thought a moment and asked, "Is this your job?"

Ruby replied, "Yes, this is my job. I am a watch dog, and I have a purpose."

Willabe asked Ruby, "Do you think I could be a watch dog?"

Ruby said, "Well, let's give it a try."

Suddenly, there was a lot of clanging and banging.

Men were running around and jumping onto the fire trucks. Willabe got in the firefighters' way.

Poor Willabe was just too small and frightened. Ruby stood guard and waited. She was on full alert.

Ruby spoke to a disappointed Willabe, "Well, at least you tried, Willabe. Maybe there is something else you can be!"

Willabe agreed and said, "Goodbye, Ruby!"

"Goodbye, Willabe!" Ruby said.

Willabe thought and thought about patient Ruby and what a good guard dog she was. She really did her job well.

I will keep trying, Willabe decided, because it's better to be a Willabe than a Wannabe.

So what will Willabe be?

25

The police station was just down the street.
Outside of the station was a parked police car.
A big brown-and-black dog sat in the back seat.

Willabe came up to the car and said, "Hello. My name is Willabe."

The big dog looked out the window and down at Willabe and said, "Hello, Willabe, my name is Samson."

Willabe asked, "What do you do here, Samson?"

Samson replied, "I help the police catch the bad guys."

Willabe thought a moment and then asked, "Is this your job?"

Samson replied, "Yes, this is my job. I am a police dog, and I have a purpose."

Willabe asked Samson, "Do you think I could be a police dog?"

Samson said, "Well, let's give it a try."

Just then, Willabe and Samson heard a lady shout.

He stole my bag!"

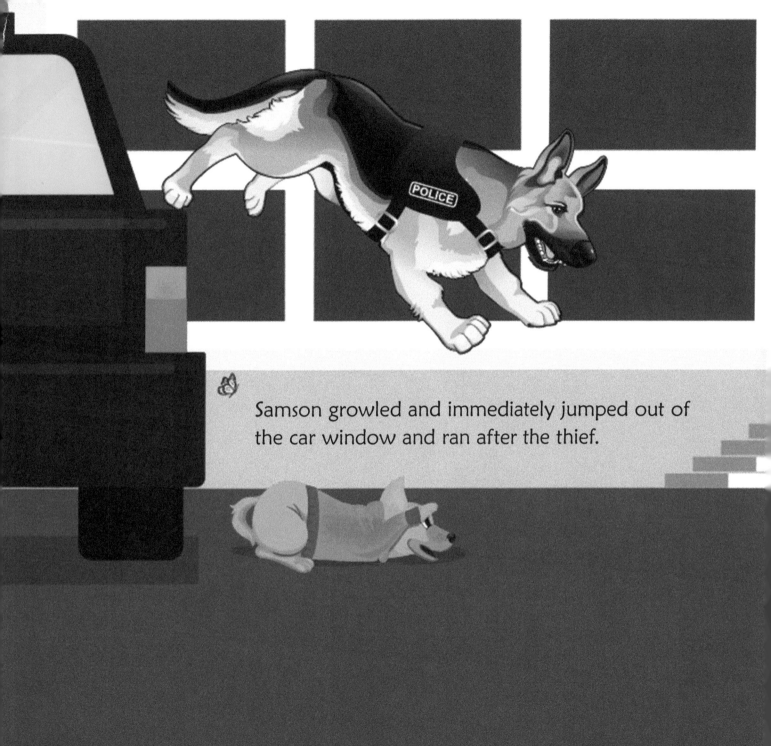

Samson growled and immediately jumped out of the car window and ran after the thief.

He leaped on the thief and took him down onto the sidewalk.

Samson waited there until the policemen ran up
to him and caught the bad guy.

Willabe could not believe his eyes!

Samson walked back to a disappointed Willabe knowing how much Willabe wanted to be like him. Samson said, "Well, at least you were willing to give it a try. Maybe there is something else you can be."

Willabe said, "Yes, I am still looking. Goodbye, Samson!"

"Goodbye, Willabe!" Samson yelled back.

Willabe thought and thought about Samson and how brave and strong he was. He really did his job well.

I will keep trying, Willabe decided, *because it's better to be a Willabe than a Wannabe.*

So what will Willabe be?

That night, Willabe thought
about all the friends he had met.

Jake was a fast herding dog,

Ruby was a patient guard dog.

Samson was a brave and strong police dog.

They all had a purpose!

I will keep trying, Willabe decided, *because it's better to be a Willabe than a Wannabe.*

So...

What will Willabe be?

Willabe will try again tomorrow

What Will Willabe Be?

Send your ideas about Willabe to

WWW.BAWILLABE.COM

Listen to The Willabe Song now available on all major music platforms

THE WILLABE SONG

CPSIA information can be obtained
at www.ICGtesting.com
Printed in the USA
LVHW072145290320
651591LV00024B/3196